The Boxcar Children Mysteries

THE BOXCAR CHILDREN
SURPRISE ISLAND
THE YELLOW HOUSE
  MYSTERY
MYSTERY RANCH
MIKE'S MYSTERY
BLUE BAY MYSTERY
THE WOODSHED MYSTERY
THE LIGHTHOUSE MYSTERY
THE MOUNTAIN TOP MYSTERY
SCHOOLHOUSE MYSTERY
CABOOSE MYSTERY
HOUSEBOAT MYSTERY
SNOWBOUND MYSTERY
TREE HOUSE MYSTERY
BICYCLE MYSTERY
MYSTERY IN THE SAND
BUS STATION MYSTERY
BENNY UNCOVERS A MYSTERY
THE HAUNTED CABIN
  MYSTERY
THE DESERTED LIBRARY
  MYSTERY
THE ANIMAL SHELTER
  MYSTERY
THE OLD MOTEL MYSTERY
THE MYSTERY OF THE HIDDEN
  PAINTING
THE AMUSEMENT PARK
  MYSTERY
THE MYSTERY OF THE MIXED-
  UP ZOO

THE CAMP-OUT MYSTERY
THE MYSTERY GIRL
THE MYSTERY CRUISE
THE DISAPPEARING FRIEND
  MYSTERY
THE MYSTERY OF THE SINGING
  GHOST
MYSTERY IN THE SNOW
THE PIZZA MYSTERY
THE MYSTERY HORSE
THE MYSTERY AT THE DOG
  SHOW
THE CASTLE MYSTERY
THE MYSTERY OF THE LOST
  VILLAGE
THE MYSTERY ON THE ICE
THE MYSTERY OF THE
  PURPLE POOL
THE GHOST SHIP MYSTERY
THE MYSTERY IN
  WASHINGTON, DC
THE CANOE TRIP MYSTERY
THE MYSTERY OF THE HIDDEN
  BEACH
THE MYSTERY OF THE MISSING
  CAT
THE MYSTERY AT SNOWFLAKE
  INN
THE MYSTERY ON STAGE
THE DINOSAUR MYSTERY
THE MYSTERY OF THE STOLEN
  MUSIC

THE MYSTERY AT THE ALAMO

created by
GERTRUDE CHANDLER WARNER

Illustrated by Charles Tang

SCHOLASTIC INC.
New York Toronto London Auckland Sydney

ISBN 0-590-95599-3

12 11 10 9 8 7 6   4 5 6 7 8 9/0

Printed in the U.S.A.   40

First Scholastic printing, April 1997

Contents

CHAPTER 1

A Visit to Texas

"We're here," Grandfather Alden said to his four grandchildren. "We're at the Alamo!"

The Boxcar Children gazed up at the old stone fort. Grandfather had told them this was one of the most famous places in all of Texas.

"And there's my friend Lew Fambles!" Grandfather smiled and headed toward the man standing outside the doors of the Alamo.

"Hello, there, Lew," Grandfather said.

"It's good to see you. These are my grand-children, Henry, Jessie, Violet, and Benny Alden."

"Welcome to Texas," Mr. Fambles said. "All you need now are some cowboy boots and a hat!"

"I'd love to have a cowboy hat!" Benny, the youngest grandchild, said. "And a horse to go with it."

"I don't think we can fit a horse on the plane," Henry, his older brother, replied. "But you can probably buy a hat."

"I want a pair of cowboy boots," Jessie said.

"Me, too," Violet added.

"We'll go shopping later," Grandfather said. "I'm sure a cowboy hat and cowboy boots will be easy to find in Texas."

"That won't be a problem at all," Mr. Fambles said.

"We're ready for our tour of the Alamo," Grandfather said, smiling at his friend.

"I'm sorry, James," Mr. Fambles said. "I'm not going to be able to give you a tour right now. There's a movie being filmed here about the history of the Alamo. They're going to use it to teach schoolchildren about Texas history. We're assisting the director as much as possible. I just got a list of things they need right away. Do you think you could find something else to do today?"

"Of course," Mr. Alden said. "There are plenty of other things to see and do here."

"Where are they filming the movie?" Jessie asked. She loved movies.

"Over there in Alamo Square," Mr. Fambles said, pointing to the crowd.

"Do you think they'd mind if we watched them?" Henry asked.

"No, not at all," Mr. Fambles said. "I watched them for a while during lunch the other day. It's really interesting to see how a movie is made."

"Well," Mr. Alden said. "I guess the movie set will be our first stop."

The children and their grandfather followed the swarm of people walking into Alamo Square. A long line of ropes separated the crowd from the movie set. Grandfather and the children moved near the movie company's props, boxes, and camera equipment.

"I can't see," Benny said.

"You can stand in front of me," Jessie said. "I've got a spot right near the set."

The movie crew was busily setting up the cameras for the next scene. Crew members bustled about.

"This is so exciting," Violet said.

Henry smiled. "I've never seen a movie being made before."

Just then, a young woman with long blond hair ran over to them. She was holding a clipboard. "I'm Amy Welsh. I'm the director of this film," the woman said.

"I'm James Alden and these are my grandchildren," Grandfather said. "We're here in San Antonio for our spring vacation. Alamo Square is our first stop."

"Well, I'm glad you got a chance to visit the set," Amy said. "The movie we're filming is called *The History of the Alamo*. It's a documentary about the Alamo from the 1800's to the present."

"I didn't know they filmed movies in Texas," Henry said.

"Oh, yes," Amy said. "Lots of movies are filmed in Texas, almost any day of the year."

"I thought most movies were filmed in Hollywood," Violet said.

"Not anymore," Amy said with a smile. "And a lot of our people working on the set are from Texas."

"That's very interesting," said Grandfather Alden.

"I wanted to speak to you because I have an idea. How old are you children?" Amy asked.

"I'm Henry and I'm fourteen."

"I'm Jessie. I'm twelve years old. And I love movies."

"I'm Benny and I'm six."

"And how about you?" Amy asked, pointing to the pretty young girl wearing a violet-colored dress.

"I'm Violet and I'm ten," she said, blushing. Violet wanted to add that she loved movies, too, but she felt shy.

"That's fabulous," Amy said. "How would

you all like to be extras in this movie? I'd need you to work three or four hours a day — from about eight o'clock in the morning until eleven or twelve. That is, if it's all right with your grandfather."

"Please, Grandfather?" begged Jessie. "Please? Let us be extras in the movie."

"Of course," Grandfather said. "I think it would be a great experience. But do you all want to work during your vacation?"

Violet nodded. "Yes, Grandfather. I think it would be fun."

Jessie twirled around in a circle. "If we're extras in a movie, that would make us movie stars!"

"Well," Henry said, "sort of."

"Do you get to eat in this movie?" asked Benny. Benny never missed an opportunity to ask about food.

"Benny," said Jessie, surprised he could find a way to work his favorite subject in no matter what they talked about.

"I just wanted to know! I still want to be in the movie even if we don't eat right away."

"If you'll be in my movie, I'll make sure you get plenty to eat. How's that?" Amy said, smiling.

"That sounds great," Benny said happily.

Grandfather Alden hugged each one of the children. "I'm going to leave you movie stars with Director Welsh."

"Please call me Amy. Everyone else does."

"Amy it is, then," Grandfather said. "I've got some work to do. I'll be back at lunch to pick you up," he said to the children. "Wait for me on that bench over there under that tree. Have fun."

"Thanks, Mr. Alden," Amy said. She gazed at the children. "Actually, I need five children for this movie."

"But there are only four of us," Benny said proudly. He was glad that he could count and read now. He remembered the first time Jessie and Violet tried to teach him to read. They had written *see* and *me* on two pieces of paper with the burned end of a stick. That was a long time ago when they had lived in the woods in the boxcar. They had been hiding from their grandfather because they thought he was a mean man. Now they lived in his beautiful house with him. But they'd loved the boxcar so much that their wonderful grandfather had it brought to his house and put it in their backyard.

"I really need another boy who's about your age, Henry," Amy said.

Henry looked around the square. He spotted a boy who looked to be around his age. "Amy, what about that boy over there? The one with the black hair and the striped shirt almost like mine. Maybe he'd like to be in a movie."

"Could you find out for me?" Amy asked. "In the meantime, I'll get your paperwork ready so you can start your movie careers."

"Sure," Jessie said.

The children hurried over to where the boy was standing.

"Hello," Henry said. "I'm Henry Alden, and these are my sisters, Jessie and Violet, and my brother, Benny. We're visiting San Antonio for the week. We're staying down the street at the Plaza Hotel."

"Hi, I'm Antonio Rivas. I live here in San Antonio."

"Your name's almost the same as the town you live in," Benny said.

"That's right," Antonio replied. "My parents named me after the town."

"We're going to be extras in this movie they're filming," Henry said. "Would you like to be an extra, too? They need one more teenager."

Benny added quickly, "They're going to buy our lunch every day."

Antonio smiled at Benny. "Sure. That sounds like fun."

"Great," Henry said. "Come with us and I'll introduce you to Amy Welsh, the director."

The children hurried across the square to find Amy.

She was sitting in a chair with the word DIRECTOR on the back.

"Amy! We found someone for you," Violet said, feeling less shy now.

"How marvelous!" Amy said, turning toward Antonio. "What is your name and how old are you?"

"I'm Antonio Rivas and I'm fourteen years old."

"Do you think you can work three or four hours a day?" Amy asked.

"Sure," Antonio said. "When can I start?"

"I want you all to fill out these forms and then we'll get going," Amy said. She passed out a pen and a set of papers to each one of them.

"I'm so excited," Jessie said as she helped Benny fill out his papers. "We're all going to be movie stars."

"Thanks for including me," Antonio said. "Some time during our work on the movie, my mother will treat us to some lemonade. She owns the stand at the edge of Alamo Square."

"That would be great," Henry said.

"It sure would," said Violet.

Amy signaled for the children to come onto to the set. She glanced at the forms they had filled out. "These look just fine. Now I want all of you to meet the other members of the cast."

The children followed Amy over to a group of people at the edge of the set. Two men and two women were talking quietly.

"Listen up, everyone," Amy said. "I want to introduce you to our extras."

Amy introduced each child. Then the other members of the cast introduced themselves.

"I'm Claire LaBelle," said a pretty blond woman.

"Claire's the star of our film," Amy explained. "She's playing the part of the grown-up Angelina Dickinson, one of the survivors of the Alamo. Angelina was just a baby when she and her mother, Susanna, were at the Alamo. Claire is also the narrator of the movie. And this is Janice Fishman, her stand-in."

"I fill in whenever Claire's unable to do

her scenes," Janice explained as she greeted the children.

"You two could almost be twins," Jessie said.

"Almost," Janice said. "Except Claire is a little bit taller."

"This is Roger Martin, our leading man," Amy said. "He's playing the part of Davy Crockett."

Henry held out his hand for a handshake. "Pleased to meet you," he said.

Roger grunted and turned away.

"Amy, I don't like children on a set," Roger said.

"You shouldn't say things like that, Roger!" Claire said. "You'll hurt their feelings."

"What about *my* feelings?" Roger said. Then he quickly went inside his trailer, slamming the door behind him.

CHAPTER 2

Trouble on the Movie Set

"I'm sorry about Roger's behavior," Claire said to the children. "This Texas heat has made him a little irritable. I'm sure you'll do a good job."

"Of course they will," said a young man with dark hair.

"This is Bob Branson," Amy said. "He's Roger Martin's stand-in. Bob's been acting since he was young."

"He sure is cute," Jessie whispered to Violet.

"Well," Amy said. "Now that everyone knows each other, let's get you kids into your costumes. Follow me to the costume tent."

"That Roger Martin seems unfriendly," Henry whispered to Jessie.

"He does," Jessie agreed. "But everyone else seems nice."

"Mary," Amy called as they neared the costume tent. "Are you in there?"

"Come on in," someone called from inside the tent.

"This is Mary Jenkins," Amy said. An older woman who was surrounded by clothes, hats, and shoes looked up from her sewing machine with a smile.

"Mary, these are our extras," Amy said as she introduced the children.

"Glad to meet you! I think I have something for everyone," Mary said as she looked through the racks of clothes that lined the wall of the tent. She quickly found long cotton dresses for the girls and shirts, pants, and hats for the boys.

"Mary keeps track of every hat, wig, shoe, and piece of clothing we use on the set," Amy explained.

"Everyone has to check costumes, wigs, jewelry, and props in and out every day," Mary said. "It's very important that you write down the time and date every time you take something. Then sign the check-out sheet by your name."

"We will," the children promised.

"When you're all dressed, we'll get started," Amy said. "Just meet me back on the set."

"Let me give you a tour," Mary said. "It will help when you come in to check out your costumes."

She showed them the collection of hats the actors used. There were hats in every shape, size, and color. Mary pulled out rack after rack of shoes and purses. Then she opened up a velvet-lined box.

"Jewels!" Violet said.

"It looks like a treasure chest," Benny said.

"They're all good fakes," Mary said,

laughing. "Most of the rings are gold-plated and most of the diamonds are really just glass and rhinestones. But when the actors wear them, it's hard to tell that they're not the real thing."

"I guess that's why they call it 'movie magic,' " Henry said.

"Exactly," Mary said. "We try to make everything look as real as possible, but it's not."

"I guess we'd better get ready now," Antonio said. "I think I heard Amy telling everyone to take their places."

"The men's dressing room is on the right," Mary said. "And the women's is on the left."

In no time at all, the children were dressed in clothing similar to what was worn in the 1800s.

"You two look really pretty," Antonio said to Jessie and Violet.

"Thanks," Jessie said. "But I'm glad we don't have to wear long skirts like these anymore."

"Me, too," Violet said.

"This hat is pretty neat," Antonio said as he looked at himself in the mirror.

"I'm glad you like your costumes," Mary said. "But make sure you turn everything in as soon as you're finished for the day. Now you'd better hurry. I'm sure Amy is ready to get started."

The children thanked Mary and rushed over to the movie set.

"There you are," Amy said. "Those costumes are perfect!"

"I feel like it's Halloween time," Benny said.

"Well, you *are* wearing a costume," Violet agreed.

Amy handed each child a script to read. Then she carefully explained what each one would be doing in the movie.

"It will take a few minutes to set up the lights," Amy said. "Then Jessie will do her part."

"Great," Jessie said. Jessie loved her part. In the first scene, she was supposed to hand a bouquet of Texas wildflowers to the leading lady, Claire LaBelle.

"Okay, places everyone," Amy yelled. "Action!"

Claire LaBelle looked beautiful in her long dress. She smiled as Jessie handed her the flowers. Claire held them up to her nose to smell the wonderful fragrance. Then, before she could say her lines, she began to sneeze uncontrollably. She struggled to speak, but she could not stop sneezing.

"Cut! Cut! Cut!" Amy shouted. "Claire! Are you all right?"

"I don't know what happened," Claire said. "I did my part just the way you told me to. But those flowers made me sneeze."

"Let me take a look at them," Bob said quickly. Claire handed him the bouquet of flowers.

Bob checked the flowers carefully while everyone looked on.

"Do you see what I see?" Violet whispered to Henry.

"The only thing I see is some pretty flowers. What do you see?" Henry asked.

"There's ragweed in that bouquet," Violet said. "Ragweed will make you sneeze if you're allergic to it."

"Maybe you should tell Amy about it, Violet," Henry said.

"Excuse me," Violet said softly. "But there are some sprigs of ragweed in that bouquet."

"Why, she's right," Bob said. He pulled the ragweed out of the bouquet and threw it away.

"How did that get in there?" Claire asked. "Everyone knows I have severe allergies."

"I'm sorry, Claire," Amy said.

"I'd be happy to film that scene for you," Janice said. "I don't have any allergies." Janice was dressed exactly like Claire.

"Thanks, Janice," Amy said. "That's very thoughtful of you."

"I can do it," Claire wheezed. "Just give me a second to catch my breath." She took a deep breath and tried to smile. "I think I can go on now."

Janice looked disappointed.

"Now everyone back to your places," Amy said, clapping her hands.

Claire and Jessie finished filming their part without any more interruptions. At the first break, Claire strolled over to the children.

"How would you all like to have a snack with me?"

"I'd love a snack," Benny answered quickly. "I mean, *we'd* love to have a snack. Thank you."

"Good!" Claire said with a smile. "I've got a surprise treat I want to share with all of you. Come with me." Then Claire led them over to her trailer, which was small and cozy, just like the Aldens' boxcar.

Jessie couldn't believe it. "Benny, doesn't this trailer remind you of our boxcar?" she asked.

"Yes, but Claire's trailer has steps and our boxcar has a stump," Benny said, smiling.

"Please open up those folding chairs and have a seat," Claire said. "I'll get the surprise."

"What do you think the surprise is?" Antonio whispered.

Before anyone could answer, Claire turned around with a tray full of cookies and a pitcher of milk. Each cookie was shaped like the state of Texas.

"Oh, how cute!" Violet said. "There's a little bluebonnet on mine."

"What's a bluebonnet?" Benny asked.

"That's the state flower of Texas," Antonio said.

"Grandfather showed us some when we were walking over to the Alamo," Jessie said. "Don't you remember, Benny?"

"He was probably too busy looking at all the food stands to notice the flowers," Henry said, smiling at his little brother.

Claire poured glasses of milk and handed out napkins.

"May I take a few cookies with me?" Benny asked. "For later, I mean."

"Of course, Benny," Claire said, laughing. "Take as many as you want."

"Thank you," Benny said happily. He

wrapped a few of the cookies in a napkin.

"Well," Claire said as she glanced at the clock. "I think we'd better get back to work. If we leave now, we'll be on the set in plenty of time. I hate to be late."

As soon as they reached the set, Amy called the children over to explain the next scene. A fake house front had been built especially for the movie. The front of the house was complete with a roof, windows, and several small wooden steps leading to a porch. Boxes of flowers and an old-fashioned rocker were on the porch. But if you opened the front door, there was nothing behind it but a small platform. Claire stood on the platform, waiting for Amy's cue to come through the door.

"That house looks real, until you look at the back of it," Jessie whispered to Violet.

"It sure does," Violet agreed.

"Listen up, everyone," Amy shouted. "In this scene, Claire will open the door and walk down those steps, carrying some books about the Alamo. After she says her lines,

Antonio and Henry will walk over to her, take the books, and exit. Does everyone understand?"

"Yes," Henry said. "That's easy."

"Great," Amy said. "Okay. Action!"

Claire opened the door and smiled. But as she started down, the second step broke with a loud cracking sound. Splinters of wood flew into the air, and Claire stumbled. The books sailed out of her hands and slid across the grass. She landed in a heap near the bottom step.

Amy ran to help Claire, followed by the children. The actress sat at the foot of the steps and rubbed her ankle.

"What happened?" Claire said, moaning. "I stepped down, and the stairs just caved in!"

"Are you hurt, Miss Claire?" Benny said.

"I think I'll be all right, dear," Claire said.

"Let me look at your ankle," Janice said, rushing through the crowd of people who had gathered around Claire. "I know first aid."

"Thank you, Janice," Claire said. "You're so thoughtful."

"I'll take a look at that step," Bob said. "One of the supports under the step probably came loose. I'll fix it right now."

"How can you tell?" Henry asked. "You can't even see underneath that step unless you rip out the top board."

"I just know about these things," Bob said.

"We have someone who can fix that, Bob," Amy said. "But thanks anyway."

"I want to fix it myself," Bob said. "That way I'll know Claire won't fall again." Bob looked over at Claire and smiled.

"Did you see that?" Violet whispered to Henry and Jessie. "I think he likes Claire. Isn't that sweet?"

"Yes," Henry agreed. "But don't you think it's kind of suspicious that all these strange things keep happening to Claire?"

"I've been thinking the same thing," Jessie said. "I heard one of the crew members say they've had a lot of things go wrong since they arrived in San Antonio."

"I think we should keep an eye out for any more accidents," Violet said. "We might have a mystery on our hands."

While the crew worked to redo the set, Henry, Benny, and Antonio walked over to watch Bob repair the step.

Jessie and Violet helped Claire hobble over to the cast members' chairs. Janice and Roger watched her as she slumped down into the chair that had her name stenciled on the back. Violet went to get Claire a glass of water.

"I'm so tired of this place," Claire said sadly. "Nothing seems to be going right. I'd do anything to get back home to California."

Jessie and Violet looked at each other. They really liked Claire and felt sorry for her.

"Claire," Roger said impatiently. "When do you think you'll be able to go on? I want to wrap this scene up as quickly as possible so I can film my scene. I'm more than ready to get out of this heat!"

"I don't think I can walk, Roger," Claire

said. "And besides, Bob is still working on the steps."

"There's no rush, Claire," Janice said quickly. "You know I'll be glad to fill in for you."

"Roger," Amy said as she waved him over to her chair, "could I speak to you for a minute?"

"What is it now?" Roger asked, walking closer to Amy.

"I've been looking over the script and I think we need to cut some of your lines from this scene. Claire needs to say more about the history of the Alamo."

"Claire, Claire, Claire. That's all I hear," Roger shouted angrily. "We're never going to complete this film if we're depending on her to carry the lead."

"Roger," Amy said quietly. "I'm trying to be fair to everyone. Claire has the lead role and it's important that she say these lines about the Alamo — "

"You're reducing my part to almost nothing!" Roger interrupted. "You won't get away with this!"

Roger walked away, muttering angrily to himself.

"Okay, everyone," Amy said, throwing her hands into the air. "It looks like we're finished for the day. We'll start again tomorrow."

Jessie and Violet went back to the house front, where Henry, Benny, and Antonio were helping Bob repair the steps.

"The supports underneath the steps were cracked," Antonio explained to the girls. "Just like Bob said they were."

"It was a lucky guess," Bob said quickly.

"We helped him fix it," Benny said. "I handed him the nails."

"You did a great job," Henry agreed.

"Wait a minute, children," Amy called. "I need to pay you before you leave for the day." She handed them ten dollars each.

"Wow," Benny said, thinking of what he would use the money for.

Violet smiled at Benny. "Why don't you save your money and buy a cowboy hat?"

"That's a good idea," Benny said as he put the money into his pocket.

"Please turn in your costumes before you go," Amy said. "I'll see you back on the set at eight o'clock tomorrow morning."

"We'll be here," Henry said.

The children quickly turned in their costumes to Mary at the costume tent. Mary carefully checked off every item and hung the clothes up.

"Everything is present and accounted for," Mary said. "I'll pin your names on your costumes so that you can get them yourselves tomorrow."

"I need to go now," Antonio said. "I'm sure my mother can use some help at the lemonade stand. I'll stop by the hotel tomorrow and we can walk to work together."

"That's a good idea," Henry said. "We'll see you in the morning."

The Boxcar Children waved good-bye to Antonio as he left to join his mother.

"Grandfather should be here soon," Jessie said. "He said to wait for him on this bench."

"I'll be glad to sit down for a while after the day we've had," Violet said.

"I think that someone is deliberately trying to keep this movie from being made," Henry said.

"Roger said he was going to get even," Jessie said. "Do you think he's the one who has been making all these accidents happen?"

"He could be," Henry said.

"Or it could be Janice," Violet said. "She really wants Claire's part. She always offers to fill in for her."

"Well," Jessie said, "that *is* her job. But it's true that if something happened to Claire, Janice would get her part."

"We should keep an eye on all of them tomorrow," Henry said. "Maybe we can figure out who's behind all this."

"Hello, there," Grandfather called out to them. "How are my movie stars?"

"Working on a movie set is fun, but it makes you really tired," Jessie said.

"And hungry!" Benny said. "Are we going someplace good to eat?"

"The hotel has a wonderful restaurant," Grandfather said.

"Then let's go to the hotel right away," Benny said. "I'm a little hungry."

"A little hungry?" Violet said, smiling.

"Okay. I'm big hungry," Benny said as he rubbed his stomach. "As big as Texas!"

"Well, we'd better be on our way, then," said Grandfather.

They all laughed as they walked to the hotel.

CHAPTER 3

Touring the Alamo

The next morning, Antonio waited for Henry, Jessie, Violet, and Benny in the hotel lobby.

"*Buenos días,*" Antonio said as the children got off the elevator.

"Good morning," Henry, Jessie, and Violet answered back.

Benny looked puzzled. "What did you say, Antonio?" he asked.

"*Buenos días,*" Antonio replied. "That means 'Good day' in Spanish."

All the children repeated the words until

they could say them correctly. Antonio taught them other Spanish words as they walked along.

As they neared Alamo Square, they could see the crew moving things around on the set.

"I hope Claire has a better day today than she did yesterday," Violet said.

"Me, too," Antonio said. "There sure have been a lot of accidents."

"If they *are* accidents," Henry said. "What if everything has been arranged on purpose to get rid of Claire?"

"Why would anyone want to do that?" Antonio asked.

"We don't know," Jessie replied. "But we're going to try to find out."

The children quickly picked up their costumes, signed the checkout sheet, and changed into their clothing.

"Hurry, now," Mary said. She was sewing the hem of one of Claire's dresses. "Amy wants to make up for lost time."

The children ran over to the set.

"Where is Claire?" Amy shouted. "We're all ready to go."

"I'm sure she has another excuse," Roger said.

"I'll go and get her," Bob offered.

"Please tell her to hurry," Amy said.

Before Bob could leave, Claire rushed onto the set. Her hair was still wet and in rollers.

"Amy, I'm sorry I'm late," Claire said breathlessly. "Someone turned my hair rollers off. It must have happened while I was in the costume tent."

"Oh, Claire," Amy said. "I was hoping things would go smoothly today."

"Me, too," Claire said. "I was up in plenty of time to get ready. I don't know how my rollers got turned off."

The children all looked at each other.

"That's okay, Claire," Janice said. "I can go on for you until your hair is dry."

"That won't be necessary," Amy said. "We can go over Claire's new lines while she fixes her hair. Then we'll start the shoot."

Janice dropped her head and walked over to her chair. She didn't look very happy.

"Do you think someone really went into Claire's trailer and turned off her rollers?" Violet asked the other children.

"It could be just an excuse for being late," Henry said.

"But Claire said she hates to be late, remember?" Jessie said. "She even made us go back a few minutes early yesterday after the break so that we would be on time."

"That's true," Henry said. "Let's watch everything that happens today. Maybe if we put our heads together we can figure out what's going on."

"Okay, people," Amy said as she walked back onto the set. "Claire's ready. Let's go."

The crew members and actors got in their places, and they finished the scenes they had begun yesterday.

"Great," Amy said when Claire finished her last line. "Let's take a fifteen-minute break while we set up the next scenes."

The children watched as the crew members set up the huge lights and the cameras for the next shots.

"Let me explain what you all will be doing in these scenes," Amy said.

This time the children's part called for them to cheer for Claire and Roger Martin, who was dressed up like Davy Crockett, one of the defenders of the Alamo. Grandfather had told them about Davy Crockett. He helped the Texans fight against Mexico, a long time ago, so Texas could be free and independent. Crockett and the other men in the Alamo lost the battle. Davy Crockett died, along with almost everyone else in the fort.

"Okay," Amy called out loudly. "Action!"

There was a loud crash. "Look!" said Benny. He pointed to a set of lights that had fallen over and shattered.

"Oh, no," said Amy. "Take a break, everyone." She hurried over to examine the broken lights. "It may take an hour or so for the camera crews to fix this mess. Well, I guess we're lucky no one was hurt."

"Why don't we go to my mother's stand and get some lemonade while we wait," Antonio suggested.

"That's a good idea," Benny said.

After returning their costumes, the children followed Antonio to his mother's lemonade stand, which was near the edge of the square. The stand was brightly decorated with red, yellow, and green streamers. A wax museum was nearby and every few minutes a loud voice boomed out the attractions inside and music played.

Antonio introduced the Aldens to his mother. "Mama," Antonio said. "These are my new friends."

"Hello, there," Mrs. Rivas said. "Antonio told me all about your adventures yesterday."

"It looks like we're going to have more adventures today," Antonio said.

"Have a glass of lemonade before you go back to being movie stars," his mother said, laughing. She handed each child a tall glass filled to the brim with her famous lemonade.

"Your mother makes the best lemonade I've ever had," Violet said.

"She does," Jessie said. "This lemonade is delicious."

"Mama," Antonio said, "would it be all right if the Aldens and their grandfather came over to our house to make *cascarones* tomorrow night?"

"That sounds like a wonderful idea," Mrs. Rivas said. "We would love for you to come."

"What's a cascarone?" Jessie asked.

"Cascarones are colored eggshells filled with confetti," Antonio said.

"Many people in Mexico and Texas make cascarones in spring," Mrs. Rivas explained. "It's a custom."

"A custom like dyeing boiled eggs at Easter and then hiding them?" Jessie asked.

"Yes," Mrs. Rivas said. "But we don't hide our cascarones after we make them."

Benny frowned. "How do you get the confetti into the eggs?"

Mrs. Rivas chuckled. "There's a trick. You'll see."

"Making cascarones sounds like fun," Violet said. "We love craft projects. We make things all the time at home."

"*¡Qué bien!* Good!" Mrs. Rivas said.

"I'm sure Grandfather will enjoy visiting your home with us," Jessie said.

"Antonio and I will be glad to pick you all up at your hotel tomorrow evening," said Mrs. Rivas.

"Great," Henry said.

"It's time to get back to work," Violet said.

"Bye, Mama," said Antonio.

"Have a good day, children," Mrs. Rivas said.

But when the children got back to the set, no one was working.

"While you were gone, another set of lights broke," Amy explained. "The crew is working on it, but it will take another couple of hours to fix it. Maybe you children should take the rest of the day off. I'll see you in the morning at eight o'clock sharp."

"We'll see you in the morning, I guess," Antonio said, sounding a little disappointed.

"Well," Violet said. "I guess we have more time to sightsee today than we thought we would have."

"Mr. Fambles is going to show us around the Alamo this afternoon," Jessie explained to Antonio.

"Then we're going sightseeing around the city. Will you come with us?" Henry asked Antonio.

"You can be our guide," Jessie said.

"I'm sorry, but I won't be able to go with you today," Antonio said. "I think I should help my mother for a while. It looks like she might have a big crowd during lunch. I want to surprise her by staying here to help. She'll be so happy."

"That sounds like a nice thing to do for your mother," said Jessie. "Maybe you can go with us some other time."

"I hope so," Antonio said. *"Buenas tardes! Good afternoon!"*

"Buenas tardes," the children called back.

Antonio waved good-bye and ran over to his mother's lemonade stand. The Boxcar Children hurried back to the hotel.

"Grandfather," Henry called as they entered the room. "Amy gave us the rest of the day off."

"That's wonderful," Mr. Alden said. "Now we can go on a tour of the Alamo and San Antonio. My friend Lew is expecting us."

"Perfect timing!" Mr. Fambles said when he saw the children and their grandfather. "I was just finishing up my paperwork."

"We're looking forward to our tour of the Alamo," Grandfather said.

"And I'm looking forward to guiding you," Mr. Fambles replied. "As the curator of the Alamo, I don't often get to walk around and give the tour myself. The tour guides usually are the ones giving the visitors the history talk."

"What does a curator do?" asked Benny.

"A curator is the person who is in charge of the artifacts of the museum," said Mr. Fambles.

"What are artifacts?" Benny asked.

"Artifacts," said Mr. Fambles, "are special

items the museum has to show from the past."

"Do you have something that belonged to Davy Crockett?" asked Benny. "He's one of my heroes."

"As a matter of fact, we do. Let me show you around," Mr. Fambles said.

The Alden children and their grandfather followed Mr. Fambles into the Alamo. They walked around while Mr. Fambles told them all about the Alamo's history.

"In 1835, during the battle for Texas independence from Mexico, San Antonio had been captured by the Texans," Mr. Fambles explained. "Only one hundred and forty-four soldiers, most of them volunteers, were left to guard the city. They were under the command of Lieutenant Colonel William B. Travis. James Bowie and Davy Crockett were among those volunteers."

"Jim Bowie. I didn't know Jim Bowie was here, too," said Henry.

"Who was Jim Bowie?" Benny asked.

"Let me tell him," Jessie said.

"Go right ahead," Mr. Fambles said. "I'm

impressed that you children know so much about Texas history already."

"Grandfather told us a lot about it before we came here," Violet said.

"Jim Bowie was the person the Bowie knife was named for," Jessie said. "Isn't that right, Grandfather?"

"That's exactly right," Grandfather said.

"Well," said Mr. Fambles, "I bet you children already know that the siege of the Alamo lasted twelve days. On the morning of March sixth, in 1836, several thousand Mexican soldiers stormed the fort. There were many deaths on both sides."

"That's sad," Violet said.

"War is always sad," Grandfather Alden said.

"Now, let me show you some of the artifacts we have here. Take a look at this," Mr. Fambles said, pointing to a glass case.

"What a beautiful little ring!" Violet said.

"Who did the ring belong to?" Jessie asked.

Mr. Fambles cleared his throat and smiled. He enjoyed telling the children this

part most of all. "There were sixteen
women and children who survived the
Alamo. Among the sixteen were Susannah
and Angelina Dickinson. The story is that
Captain Dickinson gave this ring to his
young daughter, Angelina, to wear on a ribbon around her neck for safekeeping.

"And this is the same ring?" asked Jessie.

"Yes, this is the same ring," Mr. Fambles
replied. "It's very valuable. Before you leave,
I'll tell you a little secret about it."

"Oh, boy!" Benny said. "We love se-
crets."

"What's this?" Henry asked Mr. Fambles.

"It looks like a rusty box," said Jessie.
"Why is it in a glass case?"

Everyone peered at the rusty old box and
the handled brush inside.

"This particular artifact we're not so sure
about," Mr. Fambles said. "But we think
that the box belonged to Davy Crockett,
and that this is his beard brush."

"That belonged to Davy Crockett?"
Benny asked excitedly.

"Yes," Mr. Fambles said. "Davy Crockett

might have actually brushed his beard with this very brush."

"Isn't there something else here that belonged to Davy Crockett?" Grandfather asked.

Mr. Fambles smiled as he walked along. "There sure is. This rifle supposedly was his."

All the children admired the rifle in the case. After they had seen the rest of the fort, they stopped for a few minutes in the souvenir shop.

Inside the gift shop, Benny headed straight to the Davy Crockett display.

Violet walked over to the posters and coloring crayons.

Henry, Grandfather, and Mr. Fambles went to look at the history books.

Jessie looked through the Texas cookbooks. She wanted to buy a present for Mrs. McGregor, their housekeeper.

"What are you going to buy, Grandfather?" Henry asked.

"I've already bought something," Grandfather said. "Film for my camera, and a new camera strap. I'm going to let you children take the camera with you so you can take snapshots of anything you want to remember."

"That is a great idea, James," Mr. Fambles said.

"I love taking pictures," Violet said, as she joined Henry, Grandfather, and Mr. Fambles.

"Then I'll make you the official photographer," Grandfather said as he put the camera strap around Violet's neck. "Now the camera will be easy to keep track of and you can take pictures in a snap."

"I'll keep it with me wherever I go," Violet said.

"Good," Grandfather said. "We'll have lots of wonderful pictures of our visit to Texas."

CHAPTER 4

The Secret

After their visit to the Alamo, the Boxcar Children, their grandfather, and Mr. Fambles strolled down the sidewalk and into a restaurant that Mr. Fambles had chosen. While they waited for their food, the children told their grandfather about Antonio's invitation to make cascarones.

"Of course we can go," Grandfather said. "I'm sure it will be fun."

"It was kind of the Rivas family to invite you over to their house," Mr. Fambles said. "You children have already found some good friends. Speaking of special events," he continued, "your grandfather tells me you're extras in the movie being shot in Alamo Square."

"Yes," Jessie said. "We're movie stars."

"Well," Mr. Fambles continued, "remember I told you I had a secret?"

"I remember," Benny said.

"What's the secret?" asked Jessie.

"Amy Welsh, the director of the movie, is borrowing the ring I showed you for one of the scenes," Mr. Fambles said.

"You mean the ring in the glass case that was given to little Angelina by her father?" Henry asked.

"That same ring," Mr. Fambles said. "At first I wasn't going to loan it to them because the ring is so valuable to the museum. But once your grandfather told me you children were in the movie, I decided to let them borrow it."

"You agreed to let them use it because of us?" Violet asked.

"Yes. I realized how important it is for

children to see the artifacts the museum has locked behind those glass cases. Thousands of schoolchildren will have a chance to watch the film you're making, but many of them will never get a chance to visit the Alamo."

"I didn't even know about this secret," Grandfather Alden said.

"You children will keep an eye on the ring for us, won't you?" Mr. Fambles asked.

"We sure will," Henry said.

"I've never actually had dinner with movie stars before," Mr. Fambles said. "I think this calls for a special treat. How about our famous Alamo Cream Pie?"

"Sounds great," Benny said.

"We'll all have some," Grandfather Alden said. "Thank you again for making this a special visit for me and my grandchildren."

"I've enjoyed it almost as much as they have," Mr. Fambles said.

"Let's take some pictures," Violet said.

Mr. Fambles, Grandfather Alden, Benny, Henry, and Jessie posed while Violet snapped their picture.

"I only have a couple of shots left," Violet said. "I'm going to save them so I can take pictures on the set."

"That's a wonderful thought, Violet," Grandfather said. "It will be fun to look back on the time you were Texas movie stars."

On the way back to their hotel, Henry said, "You have a nice friend, Grandfather. I really like Mr. Fambles."

"Me, too," Jessie said. "I'm so happy he's letting the movie people use the ring."

"I wonder who is going to wear it in the movie," Henry said.

"I bet it's going to be Claire LaBelle, since she's playing the part of Angelina Dickinson. That's who the ring belonged to," Violet said.

"I know she'll take care of the ring," Jessie said.

Everyone agreed.

The next morning, the Boxcar Children hurried to the set so that they wouldn't be late. They arrived a few minutes before Antonio.

"*Buenos días,*" Antonio said when he saw his friends. "Good morning."

"*Buenos días,*" the children replied.

"What is the matter?" asked Antonio, pointing to all the commotion on the set.

"I don't know," Jessie said. "We just got here, too."

Amy walked over to the children. "Good morning," she said. Then she quickly explained what each child would be doing that day.

"We're waiting for Claire," Amy said. "I have no idea where she is. We're supposed to start at eight o'clock sharp and she knows it. You didn't see her on your way over here, did you?"

"No, we didn't," Henry said.

"Do you think she's okay?" Violet asked.

"I hope so," Amy said. "She's not in her trailer or anywhere else on the set. We're three days behind schedule and if we don't finish soon, our project is going to be canceled. I've already been warned. I guess I'll just have to use Janice in her scenes this morning."

Amy walked over to Janice and spoke to her quietly. Janice smiled.

"Well, it looks like Janice is finally going to get to replace Claire," Henry said.

"I think it's awfully strange that Claire isn't on the set this morning," Jessie said.

"Why don't we go look for her," Violet suggested. "I'm sure she hasn't gone very far."

"That's a good idea," Antonio said.

The children were walking down the street when they spotted Claire eating breakfast at an outdoor café.

"Good morning, children," Claire said. "You're here awfully early."

"Claire," Jessie said, "everyone is looking for you. You were supposed to be on the set at eight!"

"What?" Claire said. "Oh, no, there's been a terrible mistake."

Claire quickly paid for her breakfast and

ran toward the set. The children followed her.

"So there you are," Amy said when Claire finally arrived. "Where have you been? You're late!"

"You called last night saying I didn't need to be on the set until nine-thirty," Claire said in a puzzled tone of voice. "I went to get breakfast."

"I didn't call you," Amy said.

"It sounded like you," Claire said. "There were announcements and some music in the background and I couldn't hear you very well, but I did hear the time clearly." Claire looked close to tears.

"Honestly, Claire. You can't be serious," Amy said angrily. "I'm telling you I didn't call you. We started at exactly eight this morning like we always do. All these delays are serious. And you seem to be causing a lot of them lately. We've decided to replace you with Janice for the next scene. We'll set up the camera shots from a distance."

Amy stormed off before Claire could say a word.

Claire looked at the children. "Honest. Someone *did* call me," Claire said, sounding upset. "I'm so unhappy. All I want to do is go home." Then Claire ran toward her trailer.

"Poor Claire," Jessie said. "I feel so sorry for her."

"Do you think someone really called her?" Henry asked.

"Of course," Violet said. "Why would she make up a story like that?"

"But you heard Claire say that she wants to go back to California," Antonio said.

"She said all she wants is to go home," Henry said.

"Yes, she did say that," Jessie admitted. "Since Violet and I aren't in these scenes, we'll go talk to Claire. We'll meet you here at break time." Then she and Violet ran over to Claire's trailer.

The sisters knocked on the door of Claire's trailer. Claire opened the door and let the girls inside.

"We came to see if we could help you," Jessie said.

"That's really sweet of you," Claire said. "But I'm afraid there's nothing anyone can do."

"Claire," Violet said. "Do you remember anything else about that call?"

"I guess it really didn't sound like Amy after all," Claire admitted. "I was really tired last night. I guess I just thought it was her since she's the only one who tells me what time to be on the set. I just remember music and loud announcements."

"That sounds familiar to me," Jessie said. "Where have we heard loud announcements?"

"At the lemonade stand," said Violet.

"That's it!" Claire said. "The wax museum plays announcements all the time."

"Whoever called must have used a pay phone near the wax museum," Jessie said.

"I just wonder why anyone would want to ruin my career," Claire said.

"So do we," Jessie said. "And we're going to find out."

CHAPTER 5

The Mysterious Stranger

When Violet and Jessie returned to the movie set, Henry, Antonio, and Benny were waiting anxiously for them.

"What did you find out?" Henry asked.

"Well, we think the call was made from a phone near Antonio's mother's lemonade stand," Violet said.

"Why do you think that?" Antonio asked.

"Because Claire kept talking about announcements and music in the background."

"*Verdad!*" Antonio said. "That's the truth!

The wax museum plays the same announcements night and day. It drives me crazy when I'm working at the booth. The pay phone is right in front of the museum and directly across from my mother's stand."

"Do you think you can keep an eye on that phone while you're working, Antonio?" Violet asked. "If the person who called Claire used that phone once, he or she might use it again."

"Of course," Antonio said.

"Okay, people," Amy said as she clapped her hands. "Break time is over. Let's make a movie here! This is an easy scene for you all to do," Amy explained to the children. "You're going to stroll down the street like you're tourists."

"Which most of us are," Henry added.

"That's right," Amy said. "When you see Claire, smile and wave at her. Then come back over here. Claire is going to talk about the number of tourists that visit San Antonio and the Alamo each year. Does anyone have any questions?"

"No," Henry said. "We understand what we're supposed to do."

"Good," Amy said. "You're all doing a great job."

As the group walked toward the set, a loud screech came from the stage.

"What in the world?" Amy said as she ran with the children in the direction of the screaming.

Mary Jenkins was on the ground crawling around the hem of Claire's wide skirt. Claire was jumping up and down, screaming.

"Help me! Help me!" Claire said as she climbed up on a chair.

"What is it?" Amy shouted.

"What's wrong, Claire?" Violet asked.

"A r-r-rat is loose in here," Claire said.

Finally Mary stood up. She was holding the tail of a squirming white mouse.

"I hate rats," Claire said. "Get that thing away from me!"

"Now, Claire, it's just a little mouse," Mary said. She gently cupped her hand over it.

"Let me have it," said Roger Martin, calmly walking over. "I'll take it to the park." He found a box with a lid and placed the mouse inside.

Claire looked embarrassed. "I'm sorry — it was silly to get so upset. Oh, dear, look at me. . . ."

Claire had ripped one sleeve of her costume and torn the hem out of her dress. Her wig had come loose and hung untidily around her shoulders. Her face was red and beaded with sweat.

"Oh, my," Mary said as she examined Claire's dress. "This costume will have to be repaired before it can be worn again."

"Claire," Amy said. "I know you're upset, but we'll have to go on without you. I can't afford any more delays. I'll just have to give your lines to Roger and Janice."

"I understand," Claire said sadly. She left the stage and ran toward her trailer.

Roger smiled. "After I get rid of this mouse, I'll be right back."

"Did you see that?" Jessie whispered to Henry. "Roger Martin seemed awfully happy when he found out he was getting some of Claire's lines."

"And he didn't look surprised when the mouse was captured, either," Henry replied.

"Do you think he put the mouse in here on purpose?" Jessie asked.

"I don't know," Henry said. "But I think we should keep an eye on him."

"I wonder where Janice is," Violet whispered. "She's usually around when we're going to film."

"That *is* unusual," Jessie said.

"I think Benny, Antonio, and I should follow Roger at lunchtime today," Henry said.

"What about our lunch?" Benny asked.

"Don't worry, Benny," Henry said. "We'll get some sandwiches and take them with us."

"That's a good idea," said Jessie. "Violet and I will keep an eye on Janice and Claire, even though I don't see how Claire could have anything to do with this."

"I hope not," Violet said. "I really like Claire."

Janice appeared on the set a few minutes before the filming started. Roger followed soon afterward. There were no accidents as they said their lines. The children did their parts perfectly.

"Okay! Cut!" Amy said. "Wonderful job, everyone! Let's go to lunch."

"It's about time some professional actors got to work around here," Roger said to Janice.

Violet and Jessie, who were standing nearby, exchanged glances.

As soon as they could leave without being noticed, Henry, Benny, and Antonio followed Roger Martin.

Jessie and Violet followed Janice. "It looks like she's going into Amy's trailer," Jessie said.

The girls ducked behind the edge of the trailer. Janice knocked on Amy's door.

"Who is it?" Amy called.

"It's me, Janice. I'm here to go over my lines."

Amy opened the door and smiled. "Great! I hope Claire will be able to film her part this afternoon, but if she can't, at least you'll be ready. Come on in. I ordered some salads for lunch."

Janice went inside and closed the door.

"Well," Violet said. "We know what Janice will be doing this afternoon. Now let's go and check on Claire."

As the girls came near Claire's trailer, her door opened and she came down the steps. Jessie grabbed Violet and dragged her behind the trailer.

"Do you think she saw us?" Violet whispered.

"I don't think so," Jessie answered. "She didn't even look around."

"Let's follow her," Violet said.

Claire headed down the street to a small café a few blocks from Alamo Square. Jessie and Violet watched through a window as she went in and sat down at a booth. After a few minutes, a tall man with red hair and glasses came in. He sat at the same table.

Jessie and Violet went into the café and snuck into the booth behind Claire and the man. Claire's back was toward the girls, and several large flowering plants shielded them from view. The girls could not see Claire or the man, but they could hear them.

"Nolan," Claire said. "You're my agent. We've worked together for years. You know that I'd love to take the starring role in that important movie being filmed in California, but I can't start right away. I can't break my contract. Once I take a job, I do the best work I can until the job is completed."

"Are you sure there's no way you can get out of this contract?" Nolan asked. "What happens if you get fired?"

Before Violet and Jessie could hear Claire's response, a waitress loudly asked what the girls wanted to order.

"Two chicken sandwiches and two glasses of milk, please," Violet said softly. The waitress wrote down their order and hurried away.

"No — I don't even want to talk about it," Claire said loudly. Then Jessie and Violet could see her heading out of the café. The man followed.

Jessie looked out the window. "They've gone their separate ways. And we still don't know what Claire said about getting fired, but we do know she wants to leave and go to California."

"Do you think she arranged all those accidents so that Amy would fire her?" Violet asked.

"I don't think so," Jessie said. "She said she does her best once she takes a job. Maybe the boys found out something that will solve this mystery."

"Are we going to stay and eat?" Violet asked as the waitress put their plates down in front of them.

"Yes," Jessie answered. "These sandwiches look delicious!"

When the girls got back to the set, the boys were waiting for them.

"You won't believe what we saw," Henry said.

"You won't believe what we heard," Jessie said.

"You go first," Henry said.

After Jessie and Violet told Henry, Benny, and Antonio about Claire's meeting with a

man named Nolan, it was the boys' turn to talk.

"We followed Roger Martin back to his trailer," Antonio said. "He met a man there. You won't believe what the man had with him!"

"What?" asked Jessie, anxious to know what the boys had seen.

"He had a cage with him," Benny said. "I saw it!"

"A cage?" Jessie said. "A cage for what?"

"It looked like a *mouse* cage. There was a treadmill inside it," Henry said.

"Are you sure?" Jessie asked.

"Yes. We're sure," Henry said. "Roger must have borrowed the mouse from a pet store. We heard him thank the man for letting him use the mouse in the movie."

"It looks like he's the one who has been making all the mischief," Antonio said.

"But why would he want to do that?" asked Violet.

"Well," Jessie said, "he doesn't like it when Claire gets most of the speaking parts, or most of the attention."

"We heard him say that. Remember?" Henry said. "He also said that he'd get even."

"You're both right," said Antonio. "But there's nothing we can do about all this today."

"Why not?" Henry asked.

"Because your grandfather is coming down the street," Antonio said with a smile. "And I need to go help my mother. I'll keep an eye on the pay phone across from our lemonade stand. Don't forget that you're coming over tonight to make cascarones. I'll meet you at your hotel after the tour."

"We haven't forgotten," Jessie said.

"We're looking forward to it," Violet said.

"Are my movie stars ready to tour San Antonio?" Grandfather said when he saw his grandchildren.

"Yes, we are!" Jessie said.

"Then let's go," Grandfather said. "We have a lot to see and do before we go over to the Rivas's house tonight."

CHAPTER 6

Sightseeing in San Antonio

The Aldens made their way onto the tour bus. The tour guide greeted everyone on board. "Good afternoon! Today we're going to visit some really great places, folks."

After a few minutes, the tour guide's voice crackled over the loudspeaker again. "That's HemisFair Plaza and the Tower of the Americas. These buildings were originally the site of San Antonio's 1968 World's Fair. We're going to stop and go inside because now it houses the Institute of Texan

Cultures. The institute traces the nationalities and history of Texas."

Grandfather Alden and the Boxcar Children followed the crowd inside the Institute of Texan Cultures.

Afterward, the tour bus stopped at the zoo and several old missions. Then it went on to the wax museum.

"I love the wax museum," Violet said. "This is my favorite display." She pointed to the wax figures of the Cowardly Lion, the Tin Man, and Dorothy with her dog, Toto.

"*The Wizard of Oz*," Henry said. "You've always loved that movie." Then Henry looked around. "Where's Benny?" he asked.

"He's over there," Violet said.

Benny was staring at an exhibit a short distance away. Henry, Violet, Jessie, and Grandfather walked over to see what he was looking at.

"Look," Benny said. "It's an exhibit about the Mexican men who fought at the Alamo. That's General Santa Anna, leader of the Mexican army."

"You're right, Benny," Jessie said.

"I know what we can do," Violet said. "We can all stand together in front of this exhibit and find someone to take our photo. Then we can develop this roll of film before we leave and give our picture to Antonio."

"That way he will never forget us," Benny said.

Grandfather Alden found a friendly-looking woman who was willing to take their photo. They all lined up in front of the exhibit and smiled.

Soon it was time to get back on the bus. The next stop was a very nice restaurant with flower baskets hanging from the ceiling.

"I think that this has been the best part of the tour so far," Benny said.

Everyone laughed.

While they ate, the Boxcar Children and their grandfather talked about all the fun they'd been having while in San Antonio.

After their meal, everyone piled onto the tour bus. It stopped right in front of the

Aldens' hotel. Antonio and his mother were waiting for them in the lobby.

"Grandfather," Henry said, "this is Antonio Rivas and his mother."

"I'm pleased to meet you both," Grandfather said as he shook hands with Antonio.

"We're glad to meet you, too," Mrs. Rivas said.

"I wish you could have come sightseeing with us," Henry said to Antonio. "We had fun."

"I would have loved to, but we were very busy at the stand," Antonio said.

Everyone got into the Rivases' van and rode to their beautiful, Spanish-style house. Dr. Rivas stood in the doorway, waiting to greet them. Antonio looked just like his father. They both had big brown eyes and warm smiles.

"Dad," Antonio said, "this is Mr. Alden."

"Pleased to meet you," Dr. Rivas said as he shook hands with Grandfather Alden.

"And these are his grandchildren, Henry, Jessie, Violet, and Benny."

"Well, well," Dr. Rivas said. "The movie-star detectives."

The children all laughed.

"Come inside and make yourselves at home," Mrs. Rivas said. She led them into a beautifully decorated room. "Please have a seat, Mr. Alden. I believe the children are going into the family room to make cascarones."

"We need to get started," Antonio said. "Cascarones are fun to make, but they take time."

Mrs. Rivas brought out four rolls of brightly colored gift wrap. "Here you are. You can use this to make the confetti."

"Making the confetti for the cascarones is more fun than buying it," Antonio explained.

He passed around pairs of scissors.

The Boxcar Children and Antonio cut the paper into little thin strips. Then they put the strips in a big cardboard box.

"You said before that you don't hide cascarones. What *do* you do with them?" Benny asked.

"I'll show you in a little while," Antonio said. "You'll just have to wait until then to find out what cascarones are good for."

"How mysterious," Henry said, smiling.

"And speaking of mysteries," Antonio said, "I almost forgot to tell you something. You'll never guess who I saw using the phone across the street from the lemonade stand."

"Who was it?" Jessie asked.

"Bob Branson," Antonio said. "Then a few minutes after he made the phone call, a man drove up. Bob got into the car with him. After they talked awhile, Bob got out and the man drove off. Then Bob headed back toward the movie set."

"Was Bob talking to a man with red hair and glasses?" Violet asked.

"Yes!" Antonio said. "He was."

"That sounds like the same man Claire had lunch with," Jessie said. "Violet and I saw them today, remember? She called him Nolan and said he was her agent."

"What's an agent?" Benny asked.

"An agent is a person who helps an actor get work," Henry explained.

"Claire has plenty of work to do," Benny said.

"You're right," Jessie said. "It seems that Claire has a choice between doing this film or a really important one in California. She can't take the job in California because she has to finish this film."

"But if she got fired from this film," Violet added, "she could take the job in California."

"I wonder why Bob was meeting with Claire's agent," Henry said.

"Maybe he's Bob's agent, too," Antonio suggested.

"I don't know," Jessie said. "But I think we need to keep an eye on Bob from now on."

"Now it's time to bring out the eggshells," Antonio said.

"What are we going to do with a bunch of eggshells?" asked Violet.

"We're going to fill them with the confetti," said Antonio. "For several weeks, every time we use an egg, we carefully break it near the top portion only. We rinse out the shell and put it right back into the egg carton. When spring comes, we fill the empty eggshells with confetti. Then we cover the hole in the shell with crepe paper and decorate it."

"So that's how you get the confetti into the shells!" Benny said. "I knew the chicken couldn't do it!"

Antonio and his mother brought in cartons of eggshells. The children stuffed the shells with confetti. Then they covered the holes with thin pieces of crepe paper and pasted them down.

"We haven't gotten to the fun part yet," Antonio said with a grin.

He brought in a big tray filled with colorful paints, glitter, ribbons, buttons, beads, seashells, glue, and paintbrushes.

Violet painted her first egg purple. Then she added a bright yellow sun. She sprinkled some glitter all over the egg and glued on a few red beads.

Jessie glued red, green, gold, and blue beads all over her gold-painted egg. Then she took a ribbon and wrapped it in a wavy pattern around the middle of the egg.

"Yours is wonderful," said Violet.

"I like your design, too," Jessie replied.

"Look at Henry's," Antonio said as he painted small birds on his egg.

Henry had painted his egg royal blue. Then he had glued different-colored buttons on it. He had also made a small hat to fit over the top of his egg.

"I think Benny gets the prize for creativity," Henry said.

Benny had painted hot dogs on his egg. He proudly held up his cascarone so everyone at the table could see it. The other children laughed and clapped their hands.

"Food is always on Benny's mind," Henry said.

"Speaking of food, I almost forgot our snack," Antonio said. "I'll be right back."

Antonio returned with a tray set with a large bowl of *queso*, or hot melted cheese, some spicy salsa, and a platter of chips. His mother brought in a pitcher of lemonade and some glasses. She looked at each one of the children's cascarones.

"You've made such unique cascarones," Mrs. Rivas said. "They're lovely. We'll let them dry. But you know, there's more to cascarones than just making them."

"What do you mean?" asked Henry.

Mrs. Rivas's eyes twinkled. "You'll just have to trust me — the best part is still to come."

"Sounds like another mystery," said Benny.

Dr. Rivas and Grandfather Alden came in to admire the cascarones.

"Children," Dr. Rivas said, "you did a fine job on these eggs. Congratulations."

"It's time to go home now," Grandfather said. "You all have a full day tomorrow."

The Rivases drove the Aldens back to their hotel.

"*Buenas noches*. Good night," Antonio said. "I'll see you on the movie set."

"Okay," Henry said. "We'll see you to-morrow."

CHAPTER 7

The Ring

"I'll be coming by the movie set today," Grandfather said to the children the next morning. "Amy has asked to use Angelina Dickinson's ring in several scenes."

"Is Mr. Fambles coming too?" Benny asked.

"Yes," Grandfather said. "He wants to make sure nothing happens to that ring. It's priceless."

"There have been a lot of mysterious things happening on that movie set," Henry said.

"If there's a mystery to be solved, I know four children who can do it," Grandfather said with a smile. "Take care and I'll see you all in a little while."

The Aldens waved good-bye to their grandfather and walked to work. When the children arrived on the movie set, they saw Amy talking to Claire.

"Claire doesn't look very happy," Violet said as they approached the two women.

"Look, why don't you two duck around the edge of those boxes and see if you can hear what's going on," Henry suggested to Violet and Jessie. "We'll go on to the costume tent."

"Good idea," Jessie said. "Maybe we'll find out something that will help us solve this mystery."

"Good morning," Violet and Jessie called out as they walked by the two women.

"Hello," Claire said. She looked close to tears.

"Hello there, girls," Amy said. "We'll be starting in just a moment. I need to finish talking with Claire."

"That's fine," Jessie said. "We don't mind waiting."

As soon as the girls were out of sight, they ducked behind a tall stack of boxes.

"Claire, my hands are tied," the girls heard Amy say. "The people who financed this film told me last night that they won't tolerate any more delays. If you can't do your part, you'll have to be replaced."

"Oh, no," Violet whispered to Jessie.

"I've been doing the best I can," Claire said. "I can't help it if these accidents keep happening."

"I realize that many of the incidents are not your fault, Claire," Amy said. "But I have to tell you that your job is hanging by a thread."

"Look, Amy," Claire said. "When I agree to do a job, I do my very best. From now on, I'm going to try even harder to make this movie a success."

"That's good to hear, Claire," Amy said. "Because if you don't, Janice Fishman will be our new leading lady. Now let's get to work." The two headed back to the set.

"Let's go, Violet," Jessie said. "They're gone now."

The girls ran to the costume tent. They quickly got their costumes, signed the checkout sheet, and rushed to change their clothes.

"Poor Claire," Violet said as she slipped into her long dress. "I feel so sorry for her."

"Well, maybe we can help her," Jessie said.

Mary walked in carrying an armful of clothes. "Good morning, girls," she said. "Did you sign out your costumes?"

"We sure did," Jessie said.

"Okay, then," Mary said. "It looks like everyone has signed for their props and costumes except for Bob Branson and Claire LaBelle."

"I'm sure they'll be in soon," Jessie said. "We're going to be filming again in a few minutes."

"Well, if everyone looks as nice as you two do, I'm sure that the film is going to be a success," Mary said, smiling.

"Let me take a picture of you in your costume, Jessie," Violet said.

"Okay," Jessie said. "Then I'll take one of you."

The sisters took turns posing for their pictures. Then they hurried to join their brothers and Antonio on the set.

"*Buenos días*, Antonio," Jessie and Violet said at the same time.

"Good morning!" Antonio said. "Your Spanish accents are improving."

"We practiced when we got up this morning," Jessie explained.

"Did you find out anything interesting from Amy and Claire?" Henry asked.

"We sure did," Violet said. "Amy told Claire that if they had any more delays, Claire would lose her job."

"We need to find out who is behind all these accidents right away," Jessie said. "It's the only way we can help Claire."

"Let's watch carefully today," Antonio said. "Maybe we can prevent any more delays from happening."

"I can help, too, Henry," Benny said.

"You sure can," Henry said. "We'll need your help."

"Jessie and I will watch Janice Fishman," Violet said.

"Aren't you forgetting someone?" Henry said.

"Who?" Violet asked.

"Claire LaBelle," Henry said. "We all hope she doesn't have anything to do with the problems on the movie set. But we don't know for sure, do we?"

"I guess you're right," Jessie said. "We'll have to keep an eye on Bob, too."

After Bob and Claire arrived, Amy came over and explained the next scene. Claire and the children would walk up to the entrance of the Alamo, and Claire would say her lines. Roger Martin, dressed as Davy Crockett, would come out of the Alamo, say a few lines, and exit. Then Claire would say that she had something special to show the children.

"I bet I know what she's going to show us," Benny said. "It's the ring that the real

Angelina Dickinson got from her father."

"You're right, Benny," Amy said. "But can you act surprised when you see it?"

"Yes," Benny said. "I'm a good actor."

"Where is Roger?" Amy asked. "He knows he is supposed to be on the set at eight o'clock sharp."

"I'll go get him," Bob said. He hurried off and returned in a few minutes, with Roger behind him.

"Roger," Amy demanded. "Where have you been?"

"I didn't see the point in getting up at the crack of dawn to say four lines," Roger said.

"That's not the point and you know it," Amy said angrily. "Please take your place. As soon as Mr. Fambles brings us the ring, we'll begin."

"Here's Mr. Fambles now," Violet said.

"Good morning, everyone," Mr. Fambles said. "Today is the big day."

"Amy told us all about the ring," Benny said. "I'm going to act surprised when I see it."

"I'm sure everyone will do a good job.

Here's the ring," Mr. Fambles said. He opened the small black box he held in his hand and held up the hammered gold ring with the cat's-eye stone.

"That's a beautiful ring," Violet said.

"It sure is," Claire agreed.

"Please be careful with it," Mr. Fambles said as he put the ring back in the box. "It's very valuable."

"I will," Claire promised as she slipped the box into her skirt pocket.

"Okay, then," Amy said. "Places, everyone. Action!"

Claire's scene with the children went smoothly. Roger Martin said his lines, and then Claire removed the ring case from her pocket. She showed the ring to the children. Then she placed a velvet ribbon through the ring and tied it around her neck. Grandfather arrived and stood with Mr. Fambles near the edge of the set watching the children. They both smiled when they saw the ring around Claire's neck.

"Cut!" Amy said, smiling. "That was excellent!"

"I acted surprised, didn't I?" Benny asked.

"You're turning into a wonderful actor," Amy replied.

Benny smiled happily.

"Okay, everyone," Amy said. "Let's take a five-minute break while we set up the next shot."

The other members of the cast and the children went over to the refreshment table to get something to eat and drink. Before Claire could leave, Violet stopped her.

"Claire," Violet said. "May I take a picture of you in front of the Alamo? You look lovely in that costume."

"Of course," Claire said, smiling. She stood in front of the doors of the Alamo. The ring glittered in the sunlight as Violet snapped the picture.

"Thank you," Violet said.

"You're welcome, dear," Claire said. "I'd love to have a copy of the picture."

"That was my last shot," Violet said. "I'll see if Grandfather can have them developed right away. Then I'll give you one."

"That would be wonderful," Claire said. "I need to go over my lines now. I'll see you back on the set in a few minutes."

Violet rewound the roll of film and ran over to where her grandfather was talking with Mr. Fambles.

"Hello, Grandfather," Violet said.

"Hello, movie star," Grandfather Alden said. "You all did a wonderful job."

"Thank you," Violet said. "Grandfather, I've used up all my film. Do you think you could have this developed and buy another roll of film for me? I'd like to give some of the pictures as gifts and take a few more before we leave."

"Of course," Grandfather said as he took the roll of film.

"There's a drugstore about a block away that will develop pictures in an hour," Mr. Fambles said. "I'm sorry I can't go with you, but I need to stay here. The next shots are going to be done inside the Alamo."

"I'll be just fine," Grandfather said. "I'll see you all in a little while."

"Thank you very much, Grandfather," Violet said. "I can't wait to see how my pictures turned out."

"I'm sure they'll come out just fine, dear," Grandfather said.

"I have to go and meet the others now," Violet said. "I think they're getting ready to get started."

"I'll be back soon with the pictures and the film," Grandfather said.

"Thank you," Violet said.

When Violet and Mr. Fambles arrived inside the Alamo, Amy was ready to begin.

"There you are," Jessie said. "I was just about to go and look for you."

"I gave my film to Grandfather so he could get my pictures developed," Violet explained.

"Good," Jessie said. "I can't wait to see them."

"Claire," Amy said, "before we get started, I just wanted to tell you that you're doing a wonderful job."

"Yes, she is," Bob Branson agreed. "I

loved the way she explained the history of Angelina Dickinson's ring. May I see it up close, Claire?"

"Of course you may," Claire said. She slipped the ribbon over her head and handed the ring to Bob.

"It's a little dark in here," Bob said. "I just want to hold it under the light." Bob walked toward the door and looked at the ring in the sunlight.

"Mr. Fambles, would you mind if we worked an extra hour inside the museum?" Amy asked. "Everything is going so smoothly, and I'd love to wrap up all the Alamo scenes today."

"Of course you may," Mr. Fambles said. "The museum doesn't open for another two hours anyway."

"Great," Amy said. "I think we may even be able to reshoot the scenes that didn't work the other day."

"Does that mean that you're not going to use the scene where I filled in for Claire?" Janice asked. She looked angry.

"Well," Amy said, "since everything today has been moving ahead of schedule, we'll have time to redo that scene."

"But that was my only real speaking part," Janice said. "Everything else was just fill-in parts."

"Maybe I can use you in another film sometime," Amy said.

"I don't think I want to wait that long," Janice said angrily. "I'll be in the trailer if you need me."

Janice hurried toward her trailer.

"What's that supposed to mean?" Jessie whispered to Violet.

"I don't know, but I've never seen Janice so upset," Violet said.

"I hope she doesn't do anything to slow the filming down," Henry said. "Claire will lose her job if anything else happens."

"Okay, everyone," Amy yelled. "Let's get back to work."

The crew members began arranging the cameras for the next scene.

"Children," Amy said, "do you think your

grandfather would mind if you worked after lunch, too?"

"I don't think he'd mind at all," Jessie said.

"He'll be back soon," Violet said. "I'm sure he'd love to watch us filming the movie. He hasn't had much time to see us at work."

"Great," Amy said. "Maybe we can wrap this film up ahead of schedule, after all."

"Here's the ring, Claire," Bob said. "Let me help you slip it on."

"Thank you, Bob," Claire said. Bob tied the ribbon that held the ring around her neck.

"Okay, children," Amy said. "In this scene, Claire will give you a tour of all the artifacts they have in the Alamo. Does everyone understand?"

The children nodded their heads. They stood in a circle around Claire.

"Okay. Action!" Amy said, clapping her hands.

Claire said her lines perfectly. The children followed her from one exhibit to the next as she explained the history of the Alamo.

"Cut! That was beautiful!" Amy said. "Everything was perfect!"

Claire smiled happily.

"Let's take a lunch break," Amy said. "Be back on the set in one hour."

"I'll see you later," Antonio said. "My father is meeting me at the lemonade stand. He's going to take me to lunch. But remember, I have a surprise for you when I come back."

"What is it?" Benny asked.

"If I tell you, it won't be a surprise," Antonio said.

"We'll see you later," Henry said to his friend.

"Would you like to go to lunch with me, Bob?" Roger asked.

"Thanks for the invitation," Bob said. "But I'm meeting someone at that little café down the street."

"Well," Roger said, "maybe some other time, then. See you later."

"Be back by one o'clock, please," Amy said.

"Of course," Roger replied. "I wouldn't dream of missing the opportunity to say the two lines you've given me in the next scene."

"Oh, Roger." Amy sighed as she shook her head. "I'll see what I can do about giving you more lines."

"You're too kind," Roger said as he left the set.

"I'll take the ring now," Mr. Fambles said to Claire.

"Of course," Claire said. She slipped the ribbon over her head and handed the ring to Mr. Fambles.

Mr. Fambles looked at the ring. His face got red.

"Oh, no," Mr. Fambles said.

"What's wrong, Mr. Fambles?" Henry asked.

"This is not Angelina Dickinson's ring," Mr. Fambles said. "This ring is a fake!"

CHAPTER 8

Lost and Found

"What do you mean?" Claire said. "That's the ring you gave me this morning!"

"No," Mr. Fambles said. "This is *not* the ring I gave you this morning."

"Wait a minute," Amy said. "What's going on here?"

"This is not Angelina Dickinson's ring," Mr. Fambles said. "Her ring is made of hammered gold and has a cat's-eye stone. This ring is gold-plated and the stone is not the same color as the real ring."

"I don't believe it!" Claire said.

"May I take a look at the ring, Mr. Fambles?" Jessie asked.

"Of course," Mr. Fambles said.

Jessie looked at the ring carefully. "This ring looks like one of the ones Mary has in the costume department."

"Maybe the rings were accidentally switched," Henry said. "The real ring may be in the jewelry chest in the costume tent."

"I don't see how that could have happened," Mr. Fambles said. "I kept the ring with me until it was time for Miss LaBelle to put it on."

"Well, I never left the set," Claire said. "I was here the whole time."

"I'm not saying you switched the rings," Henry said. "Maybe someone else switched them."

"Why don't we check with Mary," Violet suggested. "Maybe she can check her jewelry box to see if the real ring is in there."

"I hope you're right," Amy said. "This could ruin everything."

The Boxcar Children led the way to the costume tent.

"Hello, everyone," Mary said. Seeing the serious looks on their faces, she asked, "What's wrong?"

"We're missing Angelina Dickinson's ring," Mr. Fambles said.

"This is the one I've been wearing," Claire said, showing the ring to Mary. "But Mr. Fambles says it's a fake."

"That's one of our costume rings," Mary said. She quickly flipped the pages of her clipboard. "I have here that you signed it out this morning, Claire."

Everyone gathered around to look at the signature on the clipboard.

"She's right," Amy said. "Is that your signature, Claire?"

"Yes," Claire said slowly. "But I didn't sign out that ring. I was signing out my costume."

"Was anyone else in the costume tent when you were checking out your wardrobe this morning?" Violet asked.

"I don't remember seeing anyone," Claire said.

"Wait a minute," Jessie said. "It looks as if someone erased something and wrote in 'one gold ring' in its place."

"You're right," Amy said.

"I didn't have anything to do with switching those rings," Claire said, her eyes filling up with tears. "You have to believe me."

"Don't worry, Claire," Violet said. "We believe you."

"Thank you," Claire whispered.

"I'm sorry, Miss LaBelle," Mr. Fambles said. "But I will have to report this matter to the police."

"I understand," Claire said.

"Please come with me to my office," Mr. Fambles said. "I'm sure the police will want to question you."

Claire sadly followed Mr. Fambles out of the costume tent.

"I guess I'll have to call my boss," Amy said. "I'm afraid this means that Claire will no longer be working with us."

"Amy," Violet said, "could you give us an hour to try to solve this mystery before you call him?"

"I think we can help Claire if we have a little time," Henry said.

"Okay," Amy said slowly. "I'll wait one hour. But if you don't find that ring by one-thirty, I'm going to have to call my boss. I won't be able to keep it from him any longer than that."

"Thanks, Amy," Violet said.

"We'll see what we can do," Henry said.

"Maybe the ring dropped out of the box somewhere," Violet suggested as they walked along. "Let's go back to the Alamo and look around for it."

A policeman was entering the museum when the children arrived. He went inside Mr. Fambles's office. The children could see Claire, sitting with her head in her hands, through the partially opened door.

"Poor Claire," Jessie said. "I feel so sorry for her."

"There's no time to waste," Henry said. "Let's find that ring."

The children carefully searched the museum. Angelina Dickinson's ring was nowhere to be found.

"Let's think about this for a minute," Henry said. "What clues do we have?"

"Janice left in a hurry this morning," Jessie said. "She's never done that before."

"That's true," Henry said. "And Roger showed up late. He could have been up to something before he came on the set."

"You might be right," Jessie said. "He's always complaining about Claire having the largest part. Maybe he's trying to get her fired so that he can take over her lines."

"But how could anyone have had enough time to switch the rings?" Violet asked. "Mr. Fambles said that he had the ring with him until he gave it to Claire to wear."

"Wait a minute," Jessie said. "Didn't Bob ask Claire if he could look at the ring this morning?"

"He did!" Violet said. "He walked over to the door with it. How could we have forgotten?"

"I remember now," Henry said. "He said he wanted to look at the ring in the sunlight."

"Maybe he hid the ring outside," Benny said.

"I don't think he had it long enough to do that," Jessie said, "but we can look around out there."

The children searched around the front of the museum.

"It's not out here," Henry said.

"Maybe Bob was holding the fake ring in his hand the whole time," Violet said. "Then all he had to do was pocket the real ring and give Claire the fake one."

"I think you're right," Henry said. "He was the only one besides Mr. Fambles and Claire to have the ring."

"Didn't Bob say he was meeting someone at the little café down the street?" Jessie asked.

"Yes," Violet said.

"Let's go see who he's meeting," Jessie

said. "Maybe that's the person who has the real ring."

The children hurried to the café. They went inside and looked around for Bob.

"There he is," Henry said, pointing to the corner booth.

"And he's with Claire's agent," Jessie said. "The man with the red hair."

"I don't think he saw us," Jessie said. "Maybe we can sneak into the booth behind them and hear what they're saying."

The children slipped into the empty booth.

"Looks like this little event will wrap everything up, Nolan," Bob said. "I don't think Claire will be able to talk her way out of this one."

"Good," Nolan said. "We still have time to close that deal in California. We can make a lot of money if we can get Claire LaBelle for that role."

"Do you think she knows what's going on?" Bob asked.

"Of course not," Nolan said. "She would never suspect that I would try to get her fired. Claire would never break a contract. But I don't mind doing it for her if the price is right."

"Great," Bob said. "What do you want me to do with the ring?"

"Hide it somewhere," Nolan said.

"Where should I put it?" Bob asked.

"I've got a great idea. . . ." the red-haired man began.

"May I take your order?" the waitress asked the children loudly.

"Oh, no," Jessie whispered to Violet. "Not again."

"Four hot dogs and four milkshakes," Henry said quietly. "To go."

"Did you hear where Bob said he was going to hide the ring?" Jessie whispered.

"I think he said 'trailer,' " Violet said. "But I'm not sure."

"Let's wait until Bob leaves," Henry said. "Then we'll follow him."

The waitress returned with their order just as Bob and Nolan passed by. The two men were talking and didn't notice the children in the next booth. Henry quickly paid the waitress, then the children followed Bob back to the movie set.

"Let's sit on this bench for a minute," Henry said. "We don't want him to know we're following him."

"Good," Benny said. "Now I can eat my hot dog."

The children unwrapped their lunches and began to eat. Bob looked around and then he knocked on the door of Claire's trailer. He waited a few moments and then slipped inside.

"He must be hiding the ring in Claire's trailer," Violet said.

"Let's go see what he's doing," Jessie said.

"Benny," Violet said. "Grandfather must be wondering where we are. He went off to the drugstore with my film a long time ago. Could you sit here and watch for him?"

"Sure," Benny said. "I want to finish eating my lunch."

"Please tell Grandfather to meet us in Mr. Fambles's office," Henry said.

"Okay," Benny said. "I'll tell him."

"Good," Jessie said. "Let's go."

The older children ran as fast as they could to Claire's trailer. The windows were much too high for them to look through.

"I have an idea," Jessie said. "Henry, you and I can boost Violet so she'll be able to look in the window."

"Okay," Henry whispered. In a few minutes, the children looked like a human pyramid they'd seen one time in a circus. Violet was now high enough to look in the window.

"What's he doing?" Jessie whispered.

"He's putting the ring in Claire's jewelry box," Violet answered. "Quick, I've got to get down! He's coming out!"

Violet jumped down, and the children hid behind the trailer. Bob came out the door, looked around, and headed toward the movie set.

As soon as he was out of sight, the children went inside Claire's trailer.

Violet quickly found the ring inside the box. She held it tightly in her hand.

"Let's go tell Amy and Mr. Fambles what happened!" Jessie said.

"We'd better hurry," Henry said. "We only have a few minutes left before Amy calls her boss."

The children hurried over to Amy's trailer and knocked on the door.

"Amy," Henry said. "Please let us in."

"What is it?" Amy asked as she opened the door. "What's the matter?"

"We have the ring," Jessie said.

"You have the ring!" Amy said, sounding surprised. "That's the best news I've heard all day. Where is it?"

Violet gave Amy the ring.

"I'm going to return this to Mr. Fambles right now," Amy said. "Where did you find it?"

"It was in Claire's jewelry box," Violet said.

"Oh, so she *did* take it," Amy said.

"No, she didn't," Jessie said. "And we can prove it."

"You haven't called your boss yet, have you?" Violet asked.

"No, I haven't," Amy said.

"Do you think you can find Bob and

Roger and meet us in Mr. Fambles's office?" Henry asked.

"Bob and Roger?" Amy said. "What do they have to do with the missing ring?"

"We'll explain everything when you get there," Jessie said.

CHAPTER 9

The Case Is Solved

The children hurried to Mr. Fambles's office. They knocked on the door.

"Come in," Mr. Fambles said.

The police officer was still talking to Claire. He looked surprised to see the children.

"Officer Bob Small," Mr. Fambles said, "these are the Alden children. They've been acting as extras in the movie."

"Pleased to meet you," Officer Small said with a nod.

"We found the ring," Jessie said.

"And we know who took it and why," Henry added.

"You found the ring!" Mr. Fambles said. "That's wonderful news! Where is it?"

"It's right here," Amy said as she walked through the door, followed by Bob Branson and Roger Martin. She handed the ring to Mr. Fambles.

"Here they are, Grandfather," Benny said as he came running into the room.

Grandfather followed Benny into the room. "What in the world is going on here?"

"A valuable ring was stolen," Officer Small said. "But it looks like it's been found."

"Bob took it on purpose so that Claire would lose her job," Jessie said. "He's working with Nolan, Claire's agent. Someone is going to pay them both a lot of money if they can get Claire back to California in time to star in a big movie."

"Nolan and Bob planned all this?" Claire asked.

"That's right," Henry said. "Nolan said

you'd never break your contract. That's why he tried to get you fired."

"So that's why I've been having so much trouble," Claire said. "Did they let that mouse loose, too?"

"I let the mouse loose," Roger said. "I was feeling angry because I thought I deserved your part. I'm sorry. Please forgive me."

"Of course I forgive you, Roger," Claire said.

"Thank you," Roger said. He hung his head as he left the room.

"You see," Bob said. "You're trying to blame me for everything."

"That's because you're responsible for most of the mischief," Jessie said.

"We think you purposely put ragweed in Claire's bouquet and broke the supports under the steps," Violet said.

"I'll bet you were also the one who unplugged Claire's hair rollers while she was in the costume tent," Henry said.

"Bob also disguised his voice and used the pay phone across from the lemonade stand to call Claire late that night," Henry said. "He knew you'd be in a lot of trouble if you were late to work," he said to Claire.

"You don't know what you're talking about," Bob said.

"Antonio saw you using that phone," Henry said. "And we all saw you meeting Nolan."

"May I use the telephone in your secretary's office?" Claire asked Mr. Fambles.

"Of course," Mr. Fambles said.

"I'm going to tell Nolan to get over here right now. He has a lot of explaining to do."

"Bob switched the real ring with a fake one this morning," Violet explained. "Then he made it look like Claire stole it."

"I didn't do that," Bob said angrily. "Besides, you can't prove a word you've said."

"Yes, I can," Violet said. "Grandfather, do you have my pictures?"

"They're right here," Grandfather said. He handed Violet a large white envelope. Violet quickly flipped through the pictures until she found the one she was looking for.

"I took this picture of Claire right before Bob asked to look at her necklace," Violet said.

Mr. Fambles looked at the picture. He took a magnifying glass out of his desk drawer. "She's right! Claire is wearing the real ring in this picture!"

"Now I remember Bob asking Claire if he could look at the ring," Amy said. "But I never thought he would steal it."

"I didn't steal it," Bob began. "I was going to give it back." He stopped talking when he realized what he had said.

"Nolan is on his way," Claire said. "He thinks I want to talk to him because I've been fired for misplacing the ring."

"Boy," Jessie said. "He's in for a big surprise."

"I think I'd like to have a private talk with Bob while we wait for Nolan to arrive," Officer Small said. "Thanks, children, for solving this mystery."

"You're welcome," Benny said. "It was fun and I didn't even have to miss lunch."

Everyone laughed.

"I guess we'd better get back to work," Amy said. "We'll use the fake ring for any scenes we need to shoot in the future."

"Good," Mr. Fambles said. "Because I don't think I'll ever loan this ring out again."

"Are you coming, Claire?" Amy asked. "We can't start without the star of our film."

"I'm coming," Claire said with a big smile. "Thanks for everything," she said to the children. She hugged Violet, then Jessie, Henry, and Benny. "I don't know what I would have done without your help. You have some wonderful grandchildren, Mr. Alden."

"I know," said Grandfather.

Grandfather and the Boxcar Children walked back toward the movie set.

"Well," Henry said, "that mystery is solved."

"There's Antonio!" Jessie said.

"There you all are!" Antonio said. "Amy just told me what happened."

"Yes," Henry said. "The mystery is finally solved."

"I have a surprise for you," Antonio said, holding up a paper bag.

"We have one for you, too," Violet said.

"You go first," Antonio said.

Violet quickly found the picture they had taken at the wax museum.

"This is for you, Antonio," Violet said shyly. "It's something to remember us by."

"Oh, thank you," Antonio said. "Now it's my turn to surprise you." He took an egg carton filled with cascarones out of the bag he was carrying. "This is what we do with a cascarone!" He quickly smashed the decorated eggshell on top of Henry's head. Confetti spilled everywhere.

"Hey!" Henry said, laughing. "So that's why you fill them with confetti."

"That's right," Antonio said. "I guess you could say it's a smashing custom we have here in Texas."

"It sure is," Henry said, his head covered with confetti. Everyone laughed as Henry broke into a run, chasing Antonio across Alamo Square.

GERTRUDE CHANDLER WARNER discovered when she was teaching that many readers who like an exciting story could find no books that were both easy and fun to read. She decided to try to meet this need, and her first book, *The Boxcar Children*, quickly proved she had succeeded.

Miss Warner drew on her own experiences to write the mystery. As a child she spent hours watching trains go by on the tracks opposite her family home. She often dreamed about what it would be like to set up housekeeping in a caboose or freight car — the situation the Alden children find themselves in.

When Miss Warner received requests for more adventures involving Henry, Jessie, Violet, and Benny Alden, she began additional stories. In each, she chose a special setting and introduced unusual or eccentric characters who liked the unpredictable.

While the mystery element is central to each of Miss Warner's books, she never thought of them as strictly juvenile mysteries. She liked to stress the Aldens' independence and resourcefulness and their solid New England devotion to using up and making do. The Aldens go about most of their adventures with as little adult supervision as possible — something else that delights young readers.

Miss Warner lived in Putnam, Connecticut, until her death in 1979. During her lifetime, she received hundreds of letters from girls and boys telling her how much they liked her books.